THE WORLD IS ROUND

GERTRUDE STEIN

The World Is Round

Illustrated by Roberta Arenson

Unabridged

BAREFOOT BOOKS
Boston & Bath

1993

Barefoot Books
an imprint of
Shambhala Publications, Inc.
Horticultural Hall
300 Massachusetts Avenue
Boston, Massachusetts 02115

Barefoot Books Ltd
P.O. Box 95
Kingswood, Bristol 5BH

9 8 7 6 5 4 3 2 1
First Barefoot Books Edition

Series designed by Dede Cummings/IPA

Printed in China on acid-free paper ∞

Distributed in the United States by
Random House, Inc., and in Canada
by Random House of Canada Ltd

See page 147 for Library of Congress
Cataloging-in-Publication data.

CONTENTS

CONTENTS

CONTENTS

EDITOR'S PREFACE

THIS strange and wonderful book, published in 1939, is the avant-garde writer Gertrude Stein's only work for children. *The World Is Round* was inspired by a little French girl named Rose Lucie Renée Anne d'Aiguy, whom Stein and her companion Alice B. Toklas met—along with the rest of the d'Aiguy family—during a summer vacation near the village of Bilignin, France. Rose became the heroine of *The World Is Round,* and her favorite color, blue, became the book's omnipresent and all-pervading color.

In a mixture of prose and poetry, Gertrude Stein (1874–1946) tells of a girl named Rose who plays with her cousin named Willie, a dog named Love, and a lion named Billie. The main focus of the book is on Rose's perilous journey up a mountain, as she carries a hard blue garden chair on which she is determined not to sit until she arrives at the summit. Finally, alone up "there," she sings a song and suddenly becomes aware of a circling searchlight beaming onto her from a nearby hill. It is Willie who is doing the beaming. Willie and Rose, we are then told, are not really cousins after

EDITOR'S PREFACE

all; so they get married and live happily ever after.

The World Is Round has been called "a narrative for children and philosophers," for it deals playfully with the ideas of person and place, reality and identity. But it does so in a fascinating and surprising way. Gertrude Stein's writing style is known for its repetitions, syntactical discontinuities, arbitrary sequences, and associations of sounds and sense. In *The World Is Round,* she uses most of these devices with the seeming artlessness and ingenuousness of three-year-old children telling their own stories. Consider the following extract from a tale by Eliot M. (2 years, 11 months):

The daddy works in the bank. And Mommy cooks breakfast. Then we get up and get dressed. And the baby eats breakfast and honey. We go to the school and we get dressed like that. I put coat on and I go in the car. And the lion in the cage. The bear went so fast and he's going to bring the bear back, in the cage.

And then read the following from *The World Is Round:*

Her name is Rose and blue is her favorite color. But of course a lion is not blue. Rose knew that of course a lion is not blue but blue was her favorite color. . . . The lion had a name, his color was not blue but he had a name too just as any one has a name and

*his name was Billie. Willie was a boy
and Billie was a lion.*

The best way to enter the polymor-
phous perceptual realm of *The World Is
Round* is to read it aloud—a page or two
at a time, and not necessarily in sequen-
tial order. Gertrude Stein's stream-of-
consciousness—circling on itself—and
her joyous exploration of what she once
termed the "continuous present" almost
demand a kind of theatrical declaiming
of the text, perhaps accompanied with
gestures and movements on the part of
the reciter, as if one were improvising a
mime or a dance or a skit, as one takes a
long breath to read:

*But mountains yes Rose did think
about mountains and about blue*

when it was on the mountains and feathers when clouds like feathers were on the mountains and birds when one little bird and two little birds and three and four and six and seven and ten and seventeen and thirty or forty little birds all came flying and a big bird came flying and the little birds came flying and they flew higher than the big bird and they came down and one and then two and then five and then fifty of them came picking down on the head of the big bird and slowly the big bird came falling down between the mountain and the little birds all went home again . . . .

In *The World Is Round*, the author imitates and enters a child's mind in order to reveal the processes of circularity and nature of roundness. Before reaching the peak of the mountain, Rose takes a penknife and carves into a tree trunk the never-ending sentence (which Gertrude Stein had first pronounced in her 1913 story entitled "Sacred Emily"): "Rose is a rose is a rose is a rose." The first chapter of *The World Is Round* begins, "Once upon a time the world was round and you could go on it around and around"; and thirty-four chapters later, the book concludes, "[Willie and Rose] lived happily ever after and the world just went on being round."

In a study of the writings of Gertrude Stein, Donald Sutherland reminds us of a French geography book for children that begins: "The world is round like a ball, turning upon itself, and resting on nothing." *The World Is Round* is such a book, and it suggests and provides an exhilarating lightness of being.

The World Is Round was first published by William R. Scott in 1939. The text of our edition is taken from that version and includes newly commissioned illustrations by Roberta Arenson.

> JONATHAN COTT
> *Series Editor*

THE WORLD IS ROUND

ROSE IS A ROSE

ONCE upon a time the world was round and you could go on it around and around.

Everywhere there was somewhere and everywhere there they were men women children dogs cows wild pigs little rabbits cats lizards and animals. That is the way it was. And everybody dogs cats sheep rabbits and lizards and children all wanted to tell everybody all about it and they wanted to tell all about themselves.

And then there was Rose.

Rose was her name and would she have been Rose if her name had not been Rose. She used to think and then she used to think again.

Would she have been Rose if her name had not been Rose and would she have been Rose if she had been a twin.

Rose was her name all the same and her father's name was Bob and her mother's name was Kate and her uncle's name was William and her aunt's name was Gloria and her grandmother's name was Lucy. They all had names and her name was Rose, but would she have been she used to cry about it would she have been Rose if her name had not been Rose.

I tell you at this time the world was

all round and you could go on it around and around.

Rose had two dogs a big white one called Love, and a little black one called Pépé, the little black one was not hers but she said it was, it belonged to a neighbor and it never did like Rose and there was a reason why, when Rose was young, she was nine now and nine is not young no Rose was not young, well anyway when she was young she one day had little Pépé and she told him to do something, Rose liked telling everybody what to do, at least she liked to do it when she was young, now she was almost ten so now she did not tell every one what they should do but then she did and she told Pépé, and Pépé did not want to, he did not know what she wanted

him to do but even if he had he would
not have wanted to, nobody does
want to do what anybody tells them to
do, so Pépé did not do it, and Rose
shut him up in a room. Poor little
Pépé he had been taught never to do
in a room what should be done outside but he was so nervous being left
all alone he just did, poor little Pépé.
And then he was let out and there
were a great many people about but
little Pépé made no mistake he went
straight among all the legs until he
found those of Rose and then he went
up and he bit her on the leg and then
he ran away and nobody could blame
him now could they. It was the only
time he ever bit any one. And he
never would say how do you do to
Rose again and Rose always said Pépé

was her dog although he was not, so that she could forget that he never wanted to say how do you do to her. If he was her dog that was alright he did not have to say how do you do but Rose knew and Pépé knew oh yes they both knew.

Rose and her big white dog Love were pleasant together they sang songs together, these were the songs they sang.

Love drank his water and as he drank, it just goes like that like a song a nice song and while he was doing that Rose sang her song. This was her song.

I am a little girl and my name is Rose,
    Rose is my name.
Why am I a little girl

And why is my name Rose
And when am I a little girl
And when is my name Rose
And where am I a little girl
And where is my name Rose
And which little girl am I am I the
    little girl named Rose which little girl
    named Rose.

And as she sang this song and she
sang it while Love did his drinking.

Why am I a little girl
Where am I a little girl
When am I a little girl
Which little girl am I

And singing that made her so sad
she began to cry.

And when she cried Love cried he

lifted up his head and looked up at the sky and he began to cry and he and Rose and Rose and he cried and cried and cried until she stopped and at last her eyes were dried.

And all this time the world just continued to be round.

WILLIE IS WILLIE

ROSE had a cousin named Willie and once he was almost drowned. Twice he was almost drowned.

That was very exciting.

Each time was very exciting.

The world was round and there was a lake on it and the lake was round. Willie went swimming in the lake, there were three of them they were all boys swimming and there were lots of them they were all men fishing.

Lakes when they are round have

bottoms to them and there are water-
lilies pretty water-lilies white water-
lilies and yellow ones and soon very
soon one little boy and then another
little boy was caught right in by them,
water-lilies are pretty to see but they
are not pretty to feel not at all. Willie
was one and the other little boy was
the other one and the third boy was a
bigger one and he called to them to
come and they, Willie and the other
boy they couldn't come, the water-lilies did not really care but they just all
the same did not let them.

Then the bigger boy called to the
men *come and get them they cannot come
out from the water-lilies and they will
drown come and get them.* But the men
they had just finished eating and you
eat an awful lot while you are fishing

you always do and you must never go into the water right after eating, all this the men knew so what could they do.

Well the bigger boy he was that kind he said he would not leave Willie and the other behind, so he went into the water-lilies and first he pulled out one little boy and then he pulled out Willie and so he got them both to the shore.

And so Willie was not drowned although the lake and the world were both all round.

That was one time when Willie was not drowned.

Another time he was not drowned was when he was with his father and his mother and his cousin Rose they were all together.

They were going up a hill and the

rain came down with a will, you know how it comes when it comes so heavy and fast it is not wet it is a wall that is all.

So the car went up the hill and the rain came down the hill and then and then well and then there was hay, you know what hay is, hay is grass that is cut and when it is cut it is hay. Well anyway.

The hay came down the way it was no way for hay to come anyway. Hay should stay until it is taken away but this hay, the rain there was so much of it the hay came all the way and that made a dam so the water could not go away and the water went into the car and somebody opened the door and the water came more and more and Willie and Rose were there and there

was enough water there to drown
Willie certainly to drown Willie and
perhaps to drown Rose.

Well anyway just then the hay went
away, hay has that way and the water
went away and the car did stay and
neither Rose nor Willie were
drowned that day.

Much later they had a great deal to
say but they knew of course they
knew that it was true the world was
round and they were not drowned.

Now Willie liked to sing too. He
was a cousin to Rose and so it was in
the family to sing, but Willie had no
dog with whom to sing so he had to
sing with something and he sang with
owls, he could only sing in the evening but he did sing in the evening
with owls. There were three kinds of

owls a Kew owl a chuette owl and a
Hoot owl and every evening Willie
sang with owls and these are the songs
he sang.

My name is Willie I am not like Rose
I would be Willie whatever arose,
I would be Willie if Henry was my name
I would be Willie always Willie all the
  same.

And then he would stop and wait
for the owls.

Through the moon the Q. owl
blew

Who are you who are you.

Willie was not like his cousin Rose
singing did not make him cry it just
made him more and more excited.

So there was a moon and the moon
was round.

Not a sound.

Just then Willie began to sing,

Drowning
Forgetting
Remembering
I am thinking

And the chuette owl interrupted
him.

Is it
His it
Any eye of any owl is round.

Everything excited Willie, he was
more excited and he sang

Once upon a time the world was round
    the moon was round
The lake was round
And I I was almost drowned.

And the hoot owl hooted

Hullo Hullo
Willie is your name
And Willie is your nature
You are a little boy
And that is your stature
Hullo Hullo.

SILENCE

Willie was asleep
And everything began to creep
around
Willie turned in his sleep and mur-
mured
Round drowned.

EYES A SURPRISE

ROSE did not care about the moon, she liked stars.

Once some one told her that the stars were round and she wished that they had not told her.

Her dog Love did not care about the moon either and he never noticed the stars. He really did not notice the moon not even when it was all round, he liked the lights of automobiles coming in and out. That excited him and even made him bark, Love was not a barker although little Pépé was. Pépé could always bark, he really did say bow wow really he did, when you listened he really did.

Well once they were out in the evening in an automobile, not Pépé, Pépé was not Rose's dog, you remember that, but Rose and Love and the lights of the automobile were alight so who could listen to the bright moon-light, not Rose nor Love nor the rabbit, not they.

It was a little rabbit and there he was right in front and in the light and it looked as if he meant it but he really could not help it, not he not the little rabbit.

Bob, Rose's father was driving and he stopped but that did not help the little rabbit.

Light is bright and what is bright will confuse a little rabbit who has not the habit.

So the little rabbit danced from one light to the other light and could never get alright, and then Bob the father said *let out Love perhaps he will help the rabbit to run away,* so they let out the white dog Love and he saw first the light and then he saw the rabbit and he went up to say how do you do to the rabbit, that is the way Love was, he always went up and said how do you do he said it to a dog or a man or a child or a lamb or a cat or a cook or a cake or anything he just said how do you do and when he said how do you do to the little rabbit the little rabbit forgot all about the light being bright he just left that light and Love the dog

Love disappointed because the little rabbit had not said how do you do, back again, he went after him, of course any little rabbit can run quicker than any white dog and even if the white dog is nice and kind and Love is, so that was all of that. It was a lovely night and Love came back into the car and Bob the father drove on home and of course Rose sang as the rabbit ran and her song began.

> *My*
> *What a sky*
> *And then the glass pen*
> Rose did have a glass pen
> *When oh When*
> *Little glass pen*
> *Say when*
> *Will there not be that little rabbit.*

When
Then
Pen

And Rose burst into tears.

She did then she burst into tears.

A little later it was decided that Rose should go to school. She went to school where mountains were high, they were so high she never did see them. Rose was funny that way.

There at the school were other girls and Rose did not have quite as much time to sing and cry.

The teachers taught her

That the world was round

That the sun was round

That the moon was round

That the stars were round

And that they were all going around
and around

And not a sound.

It was so sad it almost made her cry

But then she did not believe it

Because mountains were so high,

And so she thought she had better
sing

And then a dreadful thing was hap-
pening

She remembered when she had
been young

That one day she had sung,

And there was a looking-glass in
front of her

And as she sang her mouth was
round and was going around and
around.

Oh dear oh dear was everything
just to be round and go around and

around. What could she do but try and remember the mountains were so high they could stop anything.

But she could not keep on remembering and forgetting of course not but she could sing of course she could sing and she could cry of course she could cry.

Oh my.

WILLIE AND HIS SINGING

ALL this time Willie was living along
    Of course he could always
make a song
    The thing that bothered Willie the
most
    Was that when there was no wind
blowing
    A twig in a bush would get going
    Just as if the wind was blowing.
    He knew when he ran
    And he knew when he sang
    And he knew who

Who was Willie
He was Willie
All through.
Willie went away not to stay.
Willie never went away to stay
That was not Willie.
But once when he went away it was
to stay there where he had seen it.
He saw it.
It was a little house and two trees
near it.
One tree sometimes makes another
tree.
Willie
Will he.
In a little while nobody wondered
that thunder rumbled in winter, light-
ning struck and thunder rumbled in
winter.
Oh Willie.

Of course Willie never went away to stay.

But Willie could sing.

Oh yes he sang a song.

He sang a little song about a house two trees and a rabbit

He sang a little song about a lizard.

A lizard climbed up the side of the house, it climbed out on the roof of the house and then the poor little lizard fell off of it.

Plump it fell off of it.

Willie saw it.

And Willie said, if the earth is all round can a lizard fall off it.

And the answer was yes if there is a roof over it.

Little lizard it lost its tail but it was not dead.

Willie sat down to rest.

It's funny he said, a lizard does not fall off a wall, it is funny and Willie sat down again to rest.

One of the things Willie did was to sit down and rest.

He liked cats and lizards, he liked frogs and pigeons he liked butter and crackers, he liked flowers and windows.

Once in a while they called for him and when they did he would talk to them.

And then he began to sing.

He sang.

Bring me bread
Bring me butter
Bring me cheese
And bring me jam
Bring me milk

And bring me chicken
Bring me eggs
And a little ham.

This is what Willie sang.
And then all at once
The world got rounder and rounder.
The stars got rounder and rounder
The moon got rounder and rounder
The sun got rounder and rounder
And Willie oh Willie was ready to drown her, not Rose dear me not Rose but his sorrows.

He loved to sing and he was exciting.

This is what Willie sang

Believe me because I tell you so
When I know yes when I know

Then I am Willie and Willie oh
Oh Willie needs Willie to tell
  them so.

Yes he said, he said *yes.*
Then Willie began to sing again.

Once upon a time I met myself
  and ran.
Once upon a time nobody saw how
  I ran.
Once upon a time something can
Once upon a time nobody sees
But I I do as I please
Run around the world just as I please.
I Willie.

Willie stopped again and again he
began to sing.

He sang.

It was time Willie did something, why not when the world was all so full anywhere, Willie went on, he saw how many there were there.

Funny said Willie that a little dog sees another little dog far far away and I, said Willie, I see a little boy.

Well well said the dog little dogs are interesting

Well well said Willie little boys are interesting.

Undoubtedly Willie had something to do and now was the time to do it.

WILLIE AND HIS LION

WILLIE had a father and Willie had a mother

That was Willie.

Willie went with his father to a little place where they sold wild animals.

If the world is round can wild animals come out of the ground.

In the place that his father took Willie wild animals did not grow there, they were not always sold there but they were always there. Everybody there had them. Wild animals were with them on the boats on the river and they went with every one in the garden and in the house. Everybody there had a wild animal and they always had them with them.

Nobody knows how the wild animals came there. If the world is round can they come out of the ground but anyway everybody had one and sometimes somebody sold one, quite often everybody sold one.

Willie's father went to get one. Which one. That was for Willie to say. It was funny seeing wild animals in a boat, one wild animal in a rowing boat, one wild animal in a sail boat, one wild animal in a motor boat.

It was a funny place this town that is it would not have been a funny place it was just like any place only

that every one always had a wild animal with them, men women and children and very often they were in the
water in a boat and the wild animal
with them and of course wild animals
are wild, of course they are wild.

It was a funny place.

Willie went everywhere so of
course he was there, beside his father
had taken him there. It was a funny
place. And Willie always took whatever he was given. So he hoped he
would have one. Any one. Everybody
had one so of course Willie would
come to have one, any wild animal
will do, if it belongs to you.

And Willie did come to have one.

Which one.

There were elephants, an elephant

in a rowing boat, Willie did not get that one.

And a tiger in a sail boat, Willie did not get that one. Willie got a lion, not a very little one, one who looked like Rose's dog Love only the Lion was terrifying. Any lion is, even a quite small one and this was a pretty big one. Willie began to sing, it was exciting and Willie sang and sang he did not sing to the lion but he sang about lions being exciting, about cats and tigers and dogs and bears about windows and curtains and giraffes and chairs. The giraffe's name was Lizzie, it really was.

Willie was so excited he almost stopped singing but as soon as he saw his own lion again he began singing

again. Singing and singing. This was
the song he sang.

Round is around.
Lions and tigers kangaroos and canaries
* abound*

They are bound to be around.
Why
Because the world is round
And they are always there.
Any little dog is afraid of there.

Then he sang in a whisper

Suppose it should rain
Suppose it should never be the same

And then Willie's voice rose

The lion is what I chose.

After a long moment he sat down to cry

He said *there, here I am just like my cousin Rose.*

Which was true

He was.

He almost was not Willie.

Oh will he again be Willie.

Not as long as he has a lion.

Not as long.

And it was getting worse and worse and then suddenly he said.

There were only two baskets of yellow peaches and I have them both.

He whispered very low.

And I have them both.

And Willie had, they were lovely round yellow peaches really round really yellow really peaches and there were only two baskets of them and Willie had them both.

And so he cheered up and decided to give the lion to his cousin Rose.

IS A LION NOT A LION

I T is not easy to give a lion away
    What did you say
    I said it is not easy to give a lion
away.

ROSE AND WILLIE'S LION

THERE is a lion its name is lion and
lion lion is its name.
Rose began to cry.
Just try
Not to make Rose cry
Just try.
That is what Willie said to the lion
When he gave Rose the lion
His lion.
Oh yes his lion.
Well there was more to it than that.
When Rose knew about a lion his

lion Willie's lion she remembered her dog Love. He was clipped like a lion but it was not that. It was when Love was only three months old and had never seen a lion.

Love was not a barker, he neither barked nor bit and when he was three months old he never had barked.

They began to be worried lest he could not bark, like children who will not talk. Well anyway.

One day Rose and her father Bob and her mother Kate and her grandmother Lucy and her uncle William were out riding and little Love was with them. Love had a pink nose and bright blue eyes and lovely white hair. When he ate asparagus and he liked to eat asparagus his rosy nose turned red with pleasure, but he never barked, not even at a cat or at asparagus. And then that day suddenly that day he stood up he was astonished and he barked. What was he astonished at. There in the middle of the open country was a big truck and on the truck were cages and the sides were down and there they were lions tigers bears and monkeys and Love just could not stand it and he barked.

Rose was very young then quite young too young then to sing a song but she sang one all the same.

This was the song she sang

How does Love know how wild they are
Wild and wild and wild they are
How does Love know who they are
When he never ever had seen them before.

And then she went on.

If a cat is in a cage
Does that make him rage.
If a dog is on a roof
Does that make him aloof
Or is there any proof
That he is a dog and on a roof.
And so
Oh
How could Love know
That wild animals were wild.
Wild animals yes wild.
Are they wild if they are wild,
If I am wild if you are wild
Are you wild oh are you wild

Rose began to cry.
She began to try
She began to deny

The wild animals could lie.

Lie quietly not die but just lie.

And then Rose once more began to sing.

I knew, she said, I knew I would sing

And this is everything.

I wish, she said, I wish I knew

Why wild animals are wild.

Why are they wild why why,

Why are they wild oh why,

And once more Rose began to cry.

Love was asleep he knew he could bark,

So why stay awake to hear Rose cry and sing

And sing and cry. Why.

That is what Love said.

Why.

And then later on when Love saw a

wild animal he sometimes did anybody sometimes did, he did not bark
he just turned his head away as much
as to say, I did once but not again, wild
animals are not interesting.

Love mostly barked in his sleep.

He dreamed.

And when he dreamed, he made a
strangled bark,

Like anybody dreaming.

Love never said whether he liked to
dream or not, but he did dream and
when he dreamed he barked.

Rose was thinking all about everything when she heard that her cousin
Willie had a lion.

ROSE THINKING

I F the world is round would a lion fall off.

A FAVORITE COLOR

ROSE certainly made a noise when no one was found

Rose oh Rose look down at the ground

And what do you see

You see that the world is not round.

That is what Rose said when she knew that it was true that a lion is not blue.

Of course she knew that a lion is not blue but blue is her favorite color.

Her name is Rose and blue is her

favorite color. But of course a lion is
not blue. Rose knew that of course a
lion is not blue but blue was her favorite color.

BRINGING BILLIE BACK

THE lion had a name, his color was not blue but he had a name too just as any one has a name and his name was Billie. Willie was a boy and Billie was a lion.

BRINGING BACK BILLIE
TO WILLIE

THAT is what happened.

Of course Rose could not keep a lion in school, she could not have kept him even if he had been blue which was her favorite color but she certainly could not keep him when he was yellow brown which is the natural color for a lion to be even if the lion has a name as well as a mane and that name is Billie.

In fact you might say really say that

Rose had never had him, the lion had never come in, of course not if a lamb can not come into a school how certainly how not can a lion.

So outside the school was a man with a drum, he was on a bicycle and the drum was on a bicycle and he was drumming and when Rose heard him drumming she went to the door and the man was calling out *either or either or, either there is a lion here or there is no lion here, either or, either or.*

Rose began to sing she just could not help herself, tears were in her eyes, she just could not help herself and she began to sing, she just could not help herself.

The drumming went on, *either or,* cried the man, *neither nor,* cried Rose *he is neither here nor there, no no lion is here no lion is there, neither nor,* cried Rose *he is neither here nor there.* The man began to drum and the drumming went further and further away and the drum was round and the wheels of the bicycle were round and they went around and around and as they went around and around the man whose mouth was round kept saying either or, either or, until there was no more no more drumming no more bicycle no more man any more.

So Rose was left at the door and she knew no more about the lion about Billie the lion than she had known before and slowly she began to sing.

Billie is going back to Willie,
Willie is getting back Billie,

No lion is blue
So there is no lion for me
There is a lion for you

Oh Willie Willie yes there is a lion for
you, a brown lion for you a real lion for
you neither will you nor will you ever know
how little I wanted to take away the lion
from you dear Willie sweet Willie take
back oh take back your lion to you, be-
cause, and she began to whisper to herself as if she herself was Willie, *because*
if a lion could be blue I would like a lion
to come from you either from you or to you
dear Willie sweet Willie there is no blue no
lion in blue no blue in lion, neither nor,
wailed Rose *neither nor,* and as she said
neither nor, there there was a door,
and filled with sobs Rose went

through the door and never any more
never any more would she remember
that it had been a lion that she saw, either or.

ONCE UPON A TIME

ONCE upon a time Willie was always there of course he was that was where Willie was and the lion he had almost forgotten that there had been a lion and he had almost forgotten that it had a name and Willie was getting very interested in knowing whether a lizard could or could not be a twin and just then he heard a bell ring and it was the lion Billie the lion back again and Willie just could not help it he just had to begin to sing and he sang a song called

Bringing Billie back again.

Bringing Billie back.

How could Billie come back.

How if there was no h in how. That is what Willie said, how could Billie come back, how, how.

And Billie was back, was Billie a lion when he was back, No said Willie, Billie was not a lion when he was back, was he a kitten when Billie was back, no said Willie Billie was not a kitten when he was back, was he a rat when he was back, no said Willie he was not a rat. Well what said Willie what was Billie when he was back, he was a twin said Willie that is what Billie was when he got back.

And Willie began to laugh and by

the time he stopped laughing he had begun again to laugh. That was Willie not Billie, Billie never had had to laugh not Billie because Billie was a lion and a lion had never had to laugh.

So that was all there was about Billie the lion and he was never there any more anywhere neither here nor there neither there nor here, Billie the lion never was anywhere. The end of Billie the lion.

A CHAIR ON THE MOUNTAIN

WHEN mountains are really true they are blue.

Rose knew they were blue and blue was her favorite color. She knew they were blue and they were far away or near just as the rain came or went away. The rain came or the rain went away any day.

And so Rose would look and see and deary me the mountains would be blue.

THE WORLD IS ROUND

And then one day she saw a mountain near and then it was all clear.

This was the way Rose knew what to say.

Listen.

Mountains are high, up there is a sky, rain is near, mountains are clear mountains are blue that is true and one mountain two mountains three mountains or four when there are mountains there always are more.

Even from the door.

So Rose would say when every day she came that way.

Rose was at school there.

There the mountains were and they were blue, oh dear blue blue just blue, dear blue sweet blue yes blue.

And then Rose began to think. It was funny about Rose she always could just begin to think. She would say to her father Bob, *Father I have a complaint to make, my dog Love does not come when I call.*

Rose was always thinking. It is easy to think when your name is Rose. Nobody's name was ever Blue, nobody's, why not. Rose never thought about that. Rose thought she thought a lot but she never did think about that.

But mountains yes Rose did think about mountains and about blue when it was on the mountains and feathers when clouds like feathers were on the mountains and birds when one little bird and two little birds and three and four and six and seven and ten and seventeen and thirty or forty little birds all came flying and a big bird

came flying and the little birds came flying and they flew higher than the big bird and they came down and one and then two and then five and then fifty of them came picking down on the head of the big bird and slowly the big bird came falling down between the mountain and the little birds all went home again. Little birds do go home again after they have scared off the big bird.

How Rose thought when she was thinking. Rose would get all round thinking her eyes her head her mouth her hands, she would get all round while she was thinking and then to relieve her hearing her thinking she would sing.

She sang a song of the mountain.

She sang,

*Dear mountain tall mountain real
mountain blue mountain yes mountain
high mountain all mountain my mountain,
I will with my chair come climbing and once
there mountain once there I will be thinking, mountain so high, who cares for the
sky yes mountain no mountain yes I will
be there.*

Tears came to her eyes.

Yes mountain she said *yes I will be
there.*

And then as she looked she saw that
one mountain had a top and the top
was a meadow and the meadow came
up to a point and on the point oh dear
yes on the point yes Rose would put a
chair and she would sit there and yes
she did care yes there she would put a
chair there there and everywhere she

would see everywhere and she would sit on that chair, yes there.

And she did and this was how she did it. All alone she did it. She and the chair there there, and it was not blue there, no dear no it was green there, grass and trees and rocks are green not blue there no blue was there but blue was her favorite color all through.

THE GOING UP WITH
THE CHAIR

THE first thing about which Rose had to make up her mind was what kind of a chair would she want way up there. She might take a camp stool that would be easiest to carry but that would not look very well up there.

She would want one that would look well way up there and that would be comfortable to sit in because she would be sitting a long time once she really did get all the way up there and

75

it would have to be one that the rain would not harm because clouds are rain and surely there would be clouds up there. No matter how many things Rose thought about there would always be some way it could be done better and a chair dear me, a chair well a chair just had to be there.

When Rose knew she had to climb and climb all the time she knew she would have to go away all day and she knew no matter how she tried that that would not do. She knew she did not know the name of the mountain she would climb she knew it had a nice name, any name is a nice name, just have it be a name and it is a nice name, but the mountain perhaps the mountain did not have a name and if it did not have a name would it be a

nice name. And if it had no name
could a chair stay there right on top of
a mountain that did not have a name.

As Rose thought of this she began
to feel very funny she just naturally did
begin to feel very very funny.

Do you suppose that Rose is a rose
If her favorite color is blue

Noses can be blue but not roses but
Rose was a rose and her favorite color
was blue.

And now she had to make up her
mind what to do.

Would the chair be a green chair or
a blue

The chair she was to take up there
There where

She was to sit on the mountain so
high

Right up under the sky

But always remember that the world is round no matter how it does sound. Remember.

So Rose had to do so many things too beside deciding whether her chair should be green or blue.

She had to think about number 142. Why.

Numbers are round.

All she took was the blue chair to go there.

It was a long way to go

And so

From morning to evening she did not get there.

But from evening to morning she did get there she and the blue chair.

THE TRIP

IT was not a trip she had to grip the blue chair and sometimes it hung by a hair not Rose's hair but any hair so great had been Rose's scare.

THIS WAS HER TRIP

S HE had decided about the chair it
was a blue chair a blue garden chair
otherwise scratches and rain and dew
and being carried all through would
do a chair harm but not a blue garden
chair.

So Rose left early so no one saw her
and her chair she held before her and
the mountain was high and so was the
sky and the world was round and was
all ground and she began to go, even
so it was a very long way to go even if

a mountain does not grow even so, climb a mountain and you will know even if there is no snow. Oh no.

Well shall I go Rose said as she was going, nobody does like to go nobody does say no and so Rose did go, even so she did go.

As she began to go it was early morning you know.

The birds began to stir

And then she heard some birds making funny screams as they flew.

And she thought of cousin Willie but that would not do.

Did the blue garden chair have arms or was it without arms, I am wondering.

UP THE HILL

A HILL is a mountain, a cow is a cat,
A fever is heating and where is
she at.

She is climbing the mountain a chair in her arms, and always around her she is full of alarms. Why not, a chair is something but not to talk to when it is too cold to be bold too hot to be cold a lot too white to be blue, too red to be wed. Oh Willie she said and there was no Willie but there was a simple noise just a noise and with a noise there were eyes and with the eyes there was a tail and then from Rose there was a wail, I wish I was not dead said Rose but if I am I will have torn my clothes, blackberries are black and blueberries are blue strawberries are red and so are you, said Rose to Rose and it was all true. She could not sit down on her chair because if she did sit down on her chair she would think she was already there and oh dear she just could not see how high it all could be but she knew oh dear yes she knew and when those birds flew she just could not do so too and she could not sing and cry no matter how much she could try because she was there right in the middle of everything that was around her and how little she could move just a little and a little and the chair was sticking and she was sticking and she could not go down because she would not know where, going down might be anywhere, going up had to be there, oh dear where was Rose she was there really she was there not stuck there but very nearly really very nearly really stuck there. And now everything began and if it had not been on a mountain and if it had not been a chair there where she was she would not care but she did not run she never ran, there was no tin can, she was not hungry oh never that, but everything helped to hold her back, but if she stayed she was afraid, run ran a chair can be a man, oh dear chair do dear chair be a man so I will not be all scare, that is what Rose said trying not to see her own hair. Dear me hair chair ran man, Rose is beginning to feel as funny as she can. Anybody try to climb a mountain all alone with only a blue garden chair to hold there and everything on a mountain that is there and then see what it is that ran. Water yes and birds yes and rats yes and snakes yes and lizards yes and cats yes and cows yes, and trees yes and scratches yes, and sticks yes, and flies yes, and bees yes but not a Rose with a chair, all a Rose with a chair can dare is just not stare but keeping on going up there.

She did.

DAY AND NIGHT

W AS she awake or did she dream
that her cousin Willie heard her
scream.

She was asleep right there with her
arms around her chair.

She never dragged the chair she carried it before and in a way it was a
cane, she leaned upon it all the same
and she went on climbing and then it
was all still, she heard a sound like a
trill and then she thought of her cousin
Willie and his lion Billie who was

never still but it was not that, no not that, it was nothing completely nothing like that, it was something moving perhaps it was just fat. It, fat can burn like that to make a trill and to be all still and to smell like the lion of cousin Will. Anything can happen while you are going up hill. And a mountain is so much harder than a hill and still. Go on.

THE NIGHT

ROSE did go on smelling and breathing and pushing and shoving and rolling, she sometimes just rolled, and moving. Anything on a mountain side is moving, rocks are rolling, stones are turning, twigs are hitting, trees are growing, flowers are showing and animals are glowing that is their eyes are and everywhere there oh dear everywhere there well Rose was there and so was her chair.

How many minutes go around to

make a second how many hours go round to make a minute how many days go around to make an hour how many nights go round to make a day and was Rose found. She never had been lost and so how could she be found even if everything did go around and around.

THE NIGHT

IT all grew rosy they call it an alpine glow when it does so but Rose well Rose is her name and blue is her favorite color.

And then she knew yes she had heard it too,

Red at night is a sailor's delight

Red in the morning is a sailor's warning,

And said she is it rose or red

And said she is it morning or evening

And said she am I awake or am I in bed,

And said she perhaps a sailor does not know perhaps somebody just told him so.

And then she remembered everything she had heard it was not about a bird it was about a spider,

A spider at night is a delight a spider in the morning is an awful warning,

And then she remembered about if you put shoes on a table it makes awful trouble, but she had not a table she only had a chair and after all she could not take off her shoes there up upon the mountain so high and that funny black that first was blue and then grey up there in the sky, and then she remembered about the moon, if you see the new moon through a window

with glass not any trouble will ever
pass no it will not and then she remembered just when she was about to
be scared that after all she had never
cared no she never had cared for any
moon so what was the use how it was
seen. And then,

Then she remembered if you see a
girl or a woman dwarf it is awful more
awful than any cough it is just awful
awful all awful and then she remembered just before she began to cry, not
that she really would cry, she only
cried when she sang, and climbing a
mountain was too occupying ever to
sing so then she remembered that it
was true if you saw a female dwarf
everything was through everything
was over there was nothing to do. And
then she remembered if she saw a boy

or a man dwarf not a fairy nothing so foolish as that but a dwarf something little that should have been big and then if she saw it and it was not a female but a man then everything would be better and better and she would get the mountain the mountain would not get her.

And just then was it a pen was it a cage was it a hut but anyway there was no but, she saw it was a dwarf, and it was not a woman it was a man and if it knew how, and it did, away it ran, so Rose oh Rose was as happy then as any hen and she fell on her chair and embraced it there the blue chair.

And then she said perhaps it was not a dwarf perhaps it was a little boy and I could have it for a toy, she knew what a little boy was because she had her cousin whose name was Willie even if he was a little silly. That is the way Rose felt about it but not on the mountain up there, there she would not care if Willie was silly if he would only be there.

NIGHT

ROSE did not want Willie, it was at night and she was not really resting and yet why did she think Willie was singing about what a day it was when Rose was not there. As she thought of that she almost let go her chair and went and went down and not up there. And then of course Willie never came. Why not when Willie was his name. Why not.

And so Rose went on again.

And now it was really night and

when she could see them the stars
were bright, and she remembered then
that they say when the stars are bright
rain comes right away and she knew it
the rain would not hurt the chair but
she would not like it to be all shiny
there. Oh dear oh dear where was that
dwarf man, it is so easy to believe
whatever they say when you are all
alone and so far away.

ROSE SAW IT CLOSE

WHAT did Rose see close, that is what she never can tell and perhaps it is just as well, suppose she did tell oh dear oh dear what she saw when she fell. Poor dear Rose. She saw it close. Never again would she stay on that spot, the chair quick the chair anywhere but there.

Rose and the chair went on, it was dark at least it would have been if it had not been so bright, alright, alright it was alright of course it was alright it was just night, that is all it was just at night.

NIGHT

What is it that water does do.
It falls it does too

It rises up that is when it is dew but when it falls, it is a water-fall and Rose knew all about that too, Rose knew almost everything that water can do, there are an awful lot when you think what, dew lakes rivers oceans fogs clouds and water-falls too, the thing that Rose heard it was night and Rose heard what she heard, dear little bird dear little water and dear little third,

not dew, not a few but a water otter, a
brown water otter, a long water otter
and Rose said not you no not you you
cannot frighten me no not you.

So then Rose was frightened all
through Rose and the chair which was
blue and the otter the brown otter,
Rose would have liked him better if
he had been blue, and then the water-
fall, the water-fall, the water-fall, the
water was full of water-fall. Rose car-
rying the chair went to look behind
there to see if there was room for the
blue chair. There always is room behind a water-fall when it is tall, and
this water-fall even in the night was
quite tall.

So Rose went in there it was all
dark darker than out there and then
she put down the chair and then she

saw she did not know but it was so, she did see it there behind the water-fall, although it was all dark there. It was written three times just how it looked as if it was done with a hair on a chair, and it said, oh dear yes it said, *Devil, Devil Devil,* it said Devil three times right there. There was no devil there of course there was no devil there there is no devil anywhere devil devil devil where. But just there where there might be a chair and writ-ten in large writing and clear in the black there, it was written there.

Dear me, Rose came out with her blue chair she decided no she would not sit down there. She decided she did not like water to fall, water fall wa-ter fall, that is what cows call but there was no cow there there was only writing there. It was too bad that Rose could read writing otherwise she would not have known that it said devil three times there. There are people who cannot read writing, but Rose was not one of them. Oh no.

So Rose and the blue chair went away from there she never could go down not there not ever again there, she could never go anywhere where water is falling and water does fall even out of a faucet, poor Rose dear Rose sweet Rose only Rose, poor Rose alone with a blue chair there.

So she went on climbing higher and higher and higher and blinking, the stars were blinking and she had to think of something. If she did not she would think of seeing that, was the Devil round, was he around, around

round, round around, oh dear no
think of Pépé, do not think of cousin
Willie, he could go around and
around, Willie did, and do not think
of the blue chair after all the seat of a
chair, might it be round oh dear
around and around, and Pépé Pépé the
little dog who bit her, no he was not
round, well his eyes were but not his
teeth, they bit oh dear she just thought
of that, they had told her that little
dogs like Pépé when there are many
they bite at the back of the legs of little
donkeys and the donkeys fall and the
little dogs eat them and do they when
they eat a donkey get round like a ball,
and there was the moon it was setting
a little flat but it was a little round oh
dear and it looked as if there was a little girl way up there in the moon with

its hair flying and partly lying and she had no chair oh dear oh dear up there.

What a place a mountain could be it looked so steep and its sides so straight and the color so blue and now one two three all out but she and red white and blue all out but you and if there was a cock it was the time when it crew, but no there was no cock, there was no hen there was no glass pen, there was only Rose, Rose Rose, Rose and all of a sudden Rose knew that in Rose there was an o and an o is round, oh dear not a sound.

THE MORNING

ROSE was a rose, she was not a dahlia, she was not a butter-cup (that is yellow), she was not a fuchsia or an oleander, well Rose wake Rose, Rose had not been asleep oh dear no, the dawn comes before the sun, and the dawn is the time to run, it is easy to run before the sun and Rose did. She was now not among the bushes which scratched but among trees which have nuts and she liked that, anybody would, and she did.

It is wonderful how many trees
there are when they are all there and
just then all the trees were all there,
tree trunks are round that is if you go
around but they are not round up into
the air. Rose drew a deep breath of re-
lief, and she lifted up her chair and she
was almost glad she was there there
where she was.

THE TREES AND THE
ROCKS UNDER THEM

THE dawn is not rosy but it is quite
cosy and in the woods it really is
so, they did once say the woods the
poor man's overcoat, and it is true
there in the woods no rain comes
through no sun comes through no
snow comes through no dust comes
through, there has to be a lot of anything before in a thick wood it does
come through, and this was so and
now Rose could know that this was so
so early in the morning before there is

a morning, and so Rose began to think
of singing she thought how nice it
would be to sing there in the woods
where there were only trees and nothing, perhaps rocks and leaves and nuts
and mushrooms but really not anything and perhaps she would like to
begin singing, singing with her blue
chair. And then she thought of course
it always did happen as soon as she began to sing she began to cry and if she
began to cry well no matter how
much she would try when she began
to sing she would begin to cry. And
then there she was in the woods, they
said the woods were a covering and
she had her blue chair and she had to
think of something but if she began to
sing or if she began to say something.
Well when you are all alone alone in

the woods even if the woods are
lovely and warm and there is a blue
chair which can never be any harm,
even so if you hear your own voice
singing or even just talking well hearing anything even if it is all your own
like your own voice is and you are all
alone and you hear your own voice
then it is frightening.

ROSE DOES SOMETHING

So Rose did not sing but she had to do something.

And what did she do well she began to smile she was climbing all the while climbing not like on a stair but climbing a little higher everywhere and then she saw a lovely tree and she thought yes it is round but all around I am going to cut *Rose is a Rose is a Rose* and so it is there and not anywhere can I hear anything which will give me a scare.

And then she thought she would
cut it higher, she would stand on her
blue chair and as high as she could
reach she would cut it there.

So she took out her pen-knife, she
did not have a glass pen she did not
have a feather from a hen she did not
have any ink she had nothing pink,
she would just stand on her chair and
around and around even if there was a
very little sound she would carve on
the tree Rose is a Rose is a Rose is a
Rose is a Rose until it went all the
way round. Suppose she said it would
not go around but she knew it would
go around. So she began.

She put the chair there she climbed
on the chair it was her blue chair but
it excited her so, not the chair but the
pen-knife and putting her name there,

that she several times almost fell off of the chair.

It is not easy to carve a name on a tree particularly oh yes particularly if the letters are round like R and O and S and E, it is not easy.

And Rose forgot the dawn forgot the rosy dawn forgot the sun forgot she was only one and all alone there she had to carve and carve with care the corners of the Os and Rs and Ss and Es in a Rose is a Rose is a Rose is a Rose.

Well first she did one and then the pen-knife seemed not to cut so well so she thought she would find a shell or a stone and if she rubbed her knife hard on it until it shone it would cut again just as it did before the knife began to groan. So she had to climb up and down on the chair and she had to find a stone and she had to go on and on, and at last well was it still dawn was there a sun well anyway at last it was more than begun it was almost done and she was cutting in the last Rose and just then well just then her eyes went on and they were round with wonder and alarm and her mouth was round and she had almost burst into a song because she saw on another tree over there that some one had been there and had carved a name and the name dear me the name was the same it was Rose and under Rose was Willie and under Willie was Billie.

It made Rose feel very funny it really did.

ROSE AND THE BELL

S HE climbed on and on and she could not tell not very well whether it was night or day but she knew it was day and not night because it was really quite bright, it might though yes it might have been night. But was it.

Well anyway she was climbing away she and the chair and she almost thought that she was almost there and then was it that she fell but anyway she did hear a bell, it was a tinkle and she

heard it clearly it might be that a stone
had stumbled and hit the garden chair,
it might be that the chair had hit
something right there or it might be
that it was a cat that had a bell or it
might be that it was a cow that had a
bell or a sheep or a bird or even a little
dog that might be running there chas-
ing a low flying crow, or it might be a
telephone, not very likely but it might,
or it might be a dinner bell, or it might
not be a bell at all it might be just a
call, or it might be a lizard or a frog or
it might be dear me it might be a log,
rolling over rocks and water, but no it
was a bell how can you tell if a bell is
a bell.

There are so many things that are
just funny it might just be silver
money, anyway Rose was there and

THE WORLD IS ROUND

she certainly did think she knew she
had heard a bell. Did she hear a bell.
And would she know it was a bell if it
was a bell. Did it come nearer and did
she go nearer and was it just perhaps
lightning and thunder.

All around the sun was shining and
the bell was ringing and the woods
were thinning and the green was shining. Please Rose please she was remembering. That is the way it was. It
made her feel a little lonesome, until
then she had been busy climbing but
now she was beginning beginning
hearing everything and it was a little
lonesome.

Rose was a little lonesome, she had
her blue chair. She was a little lonesome.

ROSE AND THE BELL

THE bell was ringing but there was no singing and Rose went climbing up and on. And then gradually she came out of the trees and there she saw an enormous green meadow going up to a point and in the middle of the meadow green, it was green as grass, there was a little black dog way up all alone and shaking himself like a dog does. Oh said Rose and she almost sat down. It was the first word she had said of all the many that had come into her head since she first began to climb. And of course it was a round one. Oh is a round one. For the first time since she began to climb Rose did not know what to do next.

ONCE UPON A TIME

ONCE upon a time way back, there were always meadows with grass on them on top of every mountain. A mountain looked as if it had rocks way up there but really way up there there was always grass and the grass always made it look elegant and it was nice.

Grass is always the most elegant more elegant than rocks and trees, trees are elegant and so are rocks but grass is more so.

And here way up there was grass and

it was going on and on and it is so much harder to climb up and up and up on grass than on rocks and under trees.

And to carry a blue chair way up there on and on through the grass because grass is steep steeper than rocks are, it was a very difficult day that day and that was the way Rose went on her way.

She had to what else could she do she had to see it through getting up there to be all the way there and to sit on her chair.

And when you are walking on grass it is harder to see where there is. And anyway what did it say. The grass did not say anyway, it was green and nothing green ever has anything to say.

Rose knew that that is why she always did prefer blue.

THE GREEN GRASS
MEADOW

ROSE was now going up and up the green grass meadow that went right on to the top. She did not say oh again she just went on. It was hot, and the green grass was hot and underneath the green grass there was ground and in that ground oh dear Rose almost stepped on it there was something round.

Rose had courage everywhere she just went on going up there.

THE LAST HOUR

IT is hard to go on when you are nearly there but not near enough to hurry up to get there. That is where Rose was and she well she hardly could go on to get there. And where was there. She almost said it she almost whispered it to herself and to the chair. Where oh where is there.

But she went on and the grass was shorter and the slant was steeper and the chair was bluer and heavier and the clouds were nearer and the top

was further because she was so near
she could not see which way it was
and if she went one way and the top
was the other way could it be that she
would never see what she could see.
Oh deary me oh deary me what did
she see. She did see and her eyes were
round with fright and her hands and
arms did hold her chair tight and suddenly green became blue and she
knew that one would become two and
three would become four and never
again no never again would there ever
be a door for her to go through.

But Rose was not like that, stum-
bling would be the beginning of tum-
bling and she would not tumble up
but tumble down if she began to
stumble and so she began to frown and
she knew she would have to begin to

count, one two one two one two one
two.

Close your eyes and count one two
open your eyes and count one two
and then green would not be blue. So
Rose began counting one two one
two and she knew that she was counting one two one two and so her eyes
were blue although her name was
Rose. Of course her eyes were blue
even though her name was Rose. That
is the reason she always did prefer blue
because her eyes were blue. And she
had two eyes and each one of her two
eyes was blue, one two one two.

And sooner than it could be true
there she saw something that was not
green nor blue, it was violet and other
colors it was high up as high as the sky
it was where she could cry it was a

rain-bow. Oh yes oh no it was a rain-bow.

And Rose just went right through, she went right through the rain-bow and she did know that was what she would do. She had it to do and she went right through the rain-bow and then there she was right on the top so that there was no other top there just the top with room for the blue chair and Rose put the blue chair there and she sat upon the chair. And Rose was there.

THERE

SHE was all alone on the top of everything and she was sitting there and she could sing.

This was the song she sang,
It began.

Here I am.
When I wish a dish
I wish a dish of ham.
When I wish a little wish
I wish that I was where I am.

She stopped and sat awhile not that she ever got up, she was so pleased with sitting she just sat.

And then she sang,

When I see I saw I can
I can see what I saw I saw where I am
*   sitting.*
Yes I am sitting.
She sighed a little.
Yes I can see I am sitting.
She sighed again.
Yes I can.
Once when five apples were red,
They never were it was my head.
No said she no it was not my head it
*   was my bed.*
So she began again.
Once when apples were red
When all is said when all is said

Are apples red
Or is it said that I know which which I have.

She stopped to think
Rose stopped to think,
I think said Rose and she wriggled a
little on her chair.
She was alone up there.
I think said Rose.
And then she began to sing.

Am I asleep or am I awake
Have I butter or have I cake,
Am I here or am I there,
Is the chair a bed or is it a chair.
Who is where.

Once more Rose began to sing.
It was getting a little dark and once
more Rose began to sing.

I am Rose my eyes are blue
I am Rose and who are you
I am Rose and when I sing
I am Rose like anything.

I am Rose said Rose and she began
to sing.

I am Rose but I am not rosy
All alone and not very cosy
I am Rose and while I am Rose
Well well Rose is Rose.

It was a little darker.
Rose sat a little tighter on her blue
chair. She really was up there. She really was.
She began to sing.

Once upon a time I knew
A chair was blue.

Once upon a time I knew whose chair
*   was blue.*
My chair was blue nobody knew but
*   I knew I knew my chair was blue.*

Rose went on singing it was getting darker. *Once upon a time there was a way to stay to stay away, I did not stay away I came away I came away away away and I am here and here is there oh where oh where is there oh where.* And Rose began to cry *oh where where where is there. I am there oh yes I am there oh where oh where is there.*

It was darker and darker and the world was rounder and rounder and the chair the blue chair was harder and harder and Rose was more there than anywhere. Oh dear yes there.

And once more Rose began to sing.

When I sing I am in a ring, and a ring is round and there is no sound and the way is white and pepper is bright and Love my dog Love he is away alright oh dear wailed Rose *oh dear oh dear I never did know I would be here, and here I am all alone all night and I am in a most awful fright. Oh chair dear chair dear hard blue chair do hold me tight I'll sit in you with all my might.*

It was getting darker and darker and there was no moon, Rose never had cared about the moon but there were lots of stars and somebody had told her that stars were round, they were not stars, and so the stars were not any comfort to her and just then well just

then what was it just then well it was
just that it was just then.

   Just then wailed Rose *I wish just then
had been a hen.*

A LIGHT

WELL it was night and night well night can be all right that is just what a night can be it can be all night. And Rose knew that. Rose knew so much it made her clutch the blue chair closer as she sat on it there.

And then just then what was it, it was not lightning it was not a moon it was not a star not even a shooting star it was not an umbrella it was not eyes eyes in the dark oh dear no it was a light, a light and oh so bright. And there it was way off on another hill and it went round and round and it went all around Rose and it was a search light surely it was and it was on a further hill and surely Will her cousin Will surely he was on another hill and he made the light go round and round and made the ground green not black and made the sky white not black and Rose oh Rose just felt warm right through to her back.

And she began to sing.

A little boy upon a hill
Oh Will oh Will.
A little boy upon a hill
He will oh will.
Oh Will oh Will.
And I am here and you are there, and I
am here and here is there and you are there

and there is here oh Will oh Will on any hill.
   Oh Will oh Will oh Will
   Oh Will oh Will.
   Will you sang Rose *oh yes you will.*

And she sang oh will oh will and she cried and cried and cried and cried and the search light went round and round and round and round.

THE END

WILLIE and Rose turned out not to be cousins, just how nobody knows, and so they married and had children and sang with them and sometimes singing made Rose cry and sometimes it made Willie get more and more excited and they lived happily ever after and the world just went on being round.

LIBRARY OF CONGRESS
CATALOGING-IN-PUBLICATION DATA

Stein, Gertrude, 1874–1946.
The world is round/Gertrude Stein.
p.   cm.—(Little barefoot books)
Summary: Rose wonders who she is, asking herself if
she would still be Rose if her name were not Rose,
and goes on a journey in search of herself.
ISBN 1-56957-905-9 (alk. paper)
[1. Identity—Fiction.]   I. Title.   II. Series.
PZ7.S821WO 1993   93-562
[E]—dc20   CIP
                        AC

UK edition: ISBN 1-898000-40-9
British Library Cataloguing-in-Publication data:
A copy of this title is available from The British Library

LITTLE BAREFOOT BOOKS

(continued on next page)

Whereyouwantogoto
and Other Unlikely Tales
by E. Nesbit
Illustrated by H. R. Millar
and Claude A. Shepperson

The World Is Round
by Gertrude Stein
Illustrated by Roberta Arenson